Christmas in America

BY CALLISTA GINGRICH
ILLUSTRATED BY SUSAN ARCIERO

★ ★ ★ ★ ★ Acknowledgments ★ ★ ★ ★ ★

Thank you to the incredible people who have made this book possible.

I especially want to thank Susan Arciero, whose outstanding illustrations have once again brought Ellis the Elephant to life.

The team at Regnery Kids has made writing *Christmas in America* a real pleasure. Thanks to Marji Ross, Cheryl Barnes, and Patricia Jackson for their insightful and creative contributions. Regnery has been remarkable in turning this book into a reality.

My sincere gratitude goes to our staff at Gingrich Productions, including Ross Worthington, Bess Kelly, Christina Maruna, Woody Hales, Audrey Bird, and John Hines. Their support has been invaluable.

Finally, I'd like to thank my husband, Newt. His enthusiasm for the Ellis the Elephant series has been my source of inspiration.

Library of Congress Control Number: 2015949951
ISBN 978-1-62157-345-6

Published in the United States by
Regnery Kids
An imprint of Regnery Publishing
A Division of Salem Media Group
300 New Jersey Ave NW
Washington, DC 20001
www.RegneryKids.com

Manufactured in the United States of America
10 9 8 7 6 5 4 3 2 1

Books are available in quantity for promotional or premium use.
For information on discounts and terms, please visit our website: www.Regnery.com.

Distributed to the trade by
Perseus Distribution
250 West 57th Street
New York, NY 10107

To my parents, Bernita and Alphonse Bisek, who taught me the true meaning of Christmas.

★ ★ ★ ★ ★

America at Christmas is a wonderful place,
full of comfort and joy and the gift of God's grace.
It's a time for remembering what matters the most,
like kindness and faith, and those we keep close.

It was Ellis the Elephant's favorite time of year,
full of wonderful stories he wanted to hear—
tales and traditions of Christmases long ago,
a cherished part of the America we know.

The story begins before our nation came to be,
with a small group of settlers and their Christmas at sea.
They'd set off from London, the new world in their sights,
to establish a colony and extend England's might.

On Christmas Day their ships were still miles from land,
so together they celebrated with what was on hand.
They prayed to meet the challenges that were in store
building the settlement of Jamestown on a distant shore.

Soon more American colonies were founded.
Up and down the coast, new cities abounded.
Christmas in Virginia was a time of good cheer,
for gathering together and traditions held dear.

They feasted on pies and drank cider till late,
while dancing and singing to help celebrate.
Ellis thought what fun it was to travel by sleigh
through Williamsburg's streets on a bright Christmas Day!

The American Revolution made Christmastime rough
for an army of Patriots fed barely enough.
On the verge of defeat after all they had tried,
General Washington needed to turn the war's tide.

He crossed the Delaware River late Christmas night,
with what remained of his army ready to fight.
In Trenton the Hessians were caught by surprise
and the Patriots' victory began the British demise.

Ellis was proud of what the Patriots achieved—
and how they built a nation on what they believed.
For independence and freedom, they'd fought a long war.
Now peace was back—and Christmas merry once more!

At George Washington's home, the party was complete
with a humpback camel for his many guests to meet.
That Christmas, Mount Vernon was a bit of a zoo.
Ellis imagined the fun of being there too!

During the great expedition of Lewis and Clark,
the long winter of 1804 was quite stark.
On the Great Plains they found shelter from the snow
with most of their journey still left to go.

Christmas morning began with a thunderous bang
as a volley of glorious cannon shots rang.
The Corps of Discovery enjoyed music and rest,
a break from their voyage deep into the west.

President Andrew Jackson was a Santa of sorts,
giving presents to orphans in need of support.
Jackson was an orphan himself as a child,
and on Christmas he wanted to make sure kids smiled.

To the White House he invited an eager young crowd
for a big Christmas "frolic"—no adults were allowed!
Children stomped gleefully through the mansion's great halls,
delighting in a fight of cotton snowballs.

The Civil War divided America in two—
the South, Confederate gray, and the North, Union blue.
The issue was slavery—would it still be allowed
in a nation that held its liberty proud?

For soldiers Christmas offered no break from the war,
nor the peace and joy of many seasons before.
But Ellis learned that some enjoyed a holiday treat—
a Christmas tree decorated with dry salted meat.

The Christmas season was happy on the frontier,
marking the end of a long and difficult year.
Pioneers worked together, helping those in need,
devoted to making their communities succeed.

Families gathered together in churches for prayer,
giving thanks to the Savior that they all shared.
They spoke of an infant, so tender and mild,
born in a manger, the holy Christ child.

President Teddy Roosevelt had a playful side,
a passion for fun that he just couldn't hide.
On Christmas he and his wife Edith were keen
to throw the best party the White House had seen.

More than five hundred children came for the day
to a great Christmas carnival, ready to play.
Exhausted from dancing and stuffed full of treats,
Ellis thought this Christmas bash couldn't be beat!

World War I took American troops overseas
to engage in a fight that left the nation displeased.
Many young soldiers spent Christmas in a trench
defending their allies—the British and the French.

In France children worried that Santa wouldn't come.
But the Americans would not let their Christmas be glum.
They collected small gifts and decorated a tree,
and gathered in a church, where their foes couldn't see.

Ellis was grateful when peace finally returned
along with the troops, their victory hard-earned.
Under President Coolidge, America was roaring—
the times were exciting, and the country was soaring.

But one thing was missing, this Ellis knew—
a national Christmas tree was long overdue.
So the president decorated a giant fir tree.
He flipped on a switch and lit up Washington, D.C.!

By the late 1920s, the boom came to an end,
leaving many Americans with no money to spend.
The Great Depression was hard and left families in fear—
Ellis thought they could use some good Christmas cheer!

Norman Rockwell was a well-known artist of the day.
With a love for America, he painted away.
He spread Christmas joy when it was needed the most,
putting Santa on the cover of the *Saturday Evening Post*.

American troops spent Christmas of 1944
in the Battle of the Bulge during the Second World War.
A few found their way to a home Christmas night
and were soon invited in for a rest from the fight.

As they sat down to eat they heard a loud knock.
It was a group of German soldiers—an alarming shock!
But in the house they agreed all fighting would cease
and together they shared a Christmas meal in peace.

On his next journey, Ellis's imagination swirled—
blasting off in Apollo 8 was out of this world!
The brave astronauts were in outer space soon,
on a mission to be the first to orbit the moon.

On Christmas Eve they broadcast a message to the nation,
reading from the Bible—the story of creation.
The astronauts sent pictures, a thousand words' worth,
along with Christmas blessings to everyone on earth.

Christmas is a time for giving thanks to God above,
for treating friends and neighbors with compassion and love.
It's a season of joy and memories to recall,
for counting our blessings, both great and small.

America is at its best this time of year,
full of charity, kindness, hope, and good cheer.
Through many challenges our nation has survived
and Americans have always kept Christmas alive.

★ ★ ★ ★ ★ Resources ★ ★ ★ ★ ★

Rockefeller Center and Plaza

Rockefeller Center is one of New York City's most famous landmarks, and the Plaza is one of the city's most iconic public spaces. The skyscraper at 30 Rockefeller Plaza is familiar to Americans as the home of NBC. Across the street, Radio City Music Hall houses the famous Rockettes, a precision dance company that has performed the Radio City Christmas Spectacular each year since the theater opened in 1932. Since 1933, a giant Christmas tree has adorned the Plaza during the holiday season. The Plaza's ice skating rink, which opened on Christmas Day in 1936, remains a tradition today.

Explore New York City at Christmas

Radio City Music Hall ★ *See the Rockettes perform their famous Radio City Christmas Spectacular.*

The Rink at Rockefeller Center ★ *Ice skate beneath the giant Christmas tree in Rockefeller Plaza.*

Jamestown Colonists' Christmas at Sea

Just before Christmas of 1606, an expedition of the Virginia Company set off from London to establish a colony in the New World. They were a crew of 105 men divided among three ships—the *Susan Constant*, the *Discovery*, and the *Godspeed*—on a mission to establish a permanent English presence in North America. The fleet spent the first six weeks of its journey trapped in the English Channel by storms that left them seasick and frustrated with their lack of progress. Yet they refused to return to shore. The men dined aboard the ships on Christmas Day. For many, it would be the final Christmas of their lives. More than half died of disease and starvation within the first few months after founding the Jamestown settlement in Virginia.

Explore Jamestown

Jamestown National Historic Site ★ *See where the Jamestown colonists established their first settlement in 1607.*

Christmas in Williamsburg

The city of Williamsburg, Virginia, was founded in 1632, and soon became one of the centers of colonial life in Virginia. The College of William and Mary was founded in the town in 1693, and six years later, Williamsburg became the capital of the Virginia Colony. The House of Burgesses met there for nearly one hundred years. Its members included George Washington, Thomas Jefferson, and Patrick Henry. At Christmas, Virginians participated in feasts, parties, and dancing balls. The holiday was a time of joy and celebration marking the birth of Jesus Christ.

Explore Colonial Williamsburg

Colonial Williamsburg ★ *Visit the historic capital city of the Virginia Colony re-created as it would have been in the eighteenth century.*

Washington Crosses the Delaware on Christmas

As Christmas of 1776 approached, the Continental Army fighting the American Revolution was on the verge of collapse. General George Washington was struggling to clothe, feed, and pay his men. Knowing that their terms of service would expire at the end of the year, he resolved to make one final, desperate attempt at a victory. Amid a heavy snow storm on Christmas night, he led his army—many men lacking boots on their feet—across the Delaware River on a nine-mile march to Trenton. There, the Patriots caught the Hessian mercenaries by surprise and achieved an improbable victory that reenergized Washington's troops and marked the turning point of the war.

Explore Washington's Crossing

Washington Crossing Historic Park ★ *See where Washington mustered his troops for the historic crossing. Reenactors conduct a river crossing in replica boats every year on Christmas Day, conditions permitting.*

Christmas at Mount Vernon

George Washington's Mount Vernon estate, settled on the Potomac River south of Alexandria, Virginia, was home to many of his Christmas celebrations from the time he began leasing the property in 1754 until his death in 1799. George and his wife, Martha, were frequent hosts. In fact, they had visitors—many uninvited and unknown travelers—virtually every night in Washington's later years (including 677 guests in 1798). Naturally, at Christmas Washington sought to provide some special entertainment. In 1787, his records indicate that he paid an Alexandria man to bring a camel to the estate for his guests to view—not out of character for the curious Washington, who showed a lifelong interest in animals.

Explore Mount Vernon

George Washington's Mount Vernon ★ *Visit Mount Vernon, Washington's estate, beautifully maintained by the Mount Vernon Ladies' Association. Each year, Aladdin the Camel is on exhibit throughout the Christmas season.*

Lewis and Clark's Christmas at Fort Mandan

The explorers of the Lewis and Clark Expedition—or the Corps of Discovery, as they were known—spent the winter of 1804 at Fort Mandan (named for the nearby villages of the Mandan tribe) in present-day North Dakota. Clark wrote in his journal that the men awoke to snowfall on a chilly Christmas morning and celebrated by firing three cannon shots. Another member of the expedition wrote that the Corps then "had the best to eat that could be had, and continued firing, dancing, and frolicking during the whole day. We enjoyed a Merry Christmas during the day and evening until nine o'clock—all in peace and quietness."

Explore Fort Mandan

The North Dakota Lewis and Clark Interpretive Center ★ *Visit the reconstruction of Lewis and Clark's Fort Mandan in Washburn, North Dakota, where the Corps of Discovery spent Christmas of 1804.*

Christmas with Andrew Jackson

Christmas was quite a production in President Andrew Jackson's White House. In 1834, Jackson threw a "frolic" for the children of the house, complete with games, music, food, and holiday treats. The highlight was an indoor "snowball" fight, waged with cotton snowballs prepared for the occasion that burst apart upon striking their target. Earlier in the day, President Jackson reportedly took the children on a trip around the nation's capital to deliver presents to local dignitaries and to visit an orphanage. The president's own parents had both died when he was young.

Explore Andrew Jackson's Life

The Hermitage ★ *Learn more about the life of President Andrew Jackson at his home, the Hermitage.*

★ ★ ★ ★ ★ Resources ★ ★ ★ ★ ★

Christmas during the Civil War

The Civil War raged from 1861 to 1865, splitting the country between the Union in the North and the seceding Confederate States of America in the South. The Southern states asserted a right to maintain the institution of human slavery without federal interference, and declared independence from the U.S. government at the outset of the war. The Union considered this secession an act of rebellion, and a long, bloody conflict followed. Christmas during the Civil War was a somber occasion. With the country torn in two, there was little joy on either side of the conflict. Anecdotes indicate that some soldiers erected small Christmas trees in front of their tents, with one soldier writing of decorating his tree with "hard tack and pork." Other reports indicate soldiers were given extra rations to mark the occasion.

Explore the Civil War

National Civil War Museum ★ *Visit the only museum devoted to teaching the complete history of the Civil War—located in Harrisburg, Pennsylvania.*

Gettysburg National Military Park ★ *See the site where one of the Civil War's most famous and important battles took place.*

Christmas on the Frontier

Beginning in the early 1800s and accelerating dramatically from the 1840s through the end of the century, millions of Americans moved west to settle the vast frontier beyond the Mississippi River. The Homestead Act of 1862 increased migration in the west even further by providing settlers with free land if they established a homestead there. Life on the frontier was difficult and not particularly exciting, so when Christmas arrived, the holiday was a welcome break. Contemporary reports from settlers describe communities coming together enthusiastically to celebrate the birth of Jesus Christ.

Explore Life on the Frontier

Museum of the Great Plains ★ *Learn about frontier life at this museum in Lawton, Oklahoma.*

Scotts Bluff National Monument ★ *Visit the annual Christmas on the Prairie event at this national monument in Nebraska to learn what the holiday was like for settlers on the frontier.*

Teddy Roosevelt's Christmas Carnival

To celebrate Christmas at the White House in 1903, President Theodore Roosevelt and his wife, Edith, hosted a spectacular Christmas "carnival." The event, attended by more than five hundred children, featured ice cream shaped like Santa Claus, among a variety of other delicacies. The party was reportedly "kids only" and was certainly among the largest holiday gatherings at the White House up to that point in American history.

Explore the Life of Theodore Roosevelt

Sagamore Hill ★ *See Teddy Roosevelt's impressive home, Sagamore Hill, in Oyster Bay, New York.*

Theodore Roosevelt Birthplace ★ *Tour the New York City townhome where President Roosevelt was born and raised.*

Christmas with the 168th Infantry/ World War I

When the United States entered World War I in the spring of 1917, the men of the 168th Infantry were sent to a small village in northern France. Even though the soldiers did not speak the same language as the local people, they managed to become friendly. By Christmas of that year, the men decided to surprise the children of the village with a party. They obtained a Christmas tree and whatever presents they could find, and gathered the local children in the church on Christmas Eve, where Santa Claus was waiting for them. The American soldiers made Christmas a little happier for the young French villagers who had endured three Christmases of war already.

Explore World War I

National World War I Museum ★ *Learn about World War I at Liberty Memorial in Kansas City, Missouri.*

First National Christmas Tree

Although Christmas trees were often displayed inside the White House during previous holiday seasons, our nation's capital had no official national Christmas tree until 1923. On Christmas Eve of that year, President Coolidge, joined by his wife, Grace, pressed a button to light up a forty-eight-foot balsam fir on the ellipse in front of the White House. The tree had been brought for the occasion from Vermont, Coolidge's home state. The U.S. Marine Corps Band played at the ceremony—an event that continues each year to this day, not far from where President Coolidge lit the first national Christmas tree nearly a century ago.

Explore the First National Christmas Tree

President's Park ★ *Tour the White House grounds and gardens to see where President Coolidge lit the first national Christmas tree.*

President Calvin Coolidge Homestead ★ *See where President Coolidge was born and raised in the small village of Plymouth Notch, Vermont.*

Norman Rockwell

Norman Rockwell was one of the most iconic and popular artists in American history. His paintings and illustrations of American life helped define the nation's self image in the twentieth century, most famously on covers of the *Saturday Evening Post*. Over a period of nearly fifty years, Rockwell painted more than three hundred cover images, including depictions of life during the Great Depression, World War II, and of course, Christmas. Rockwell produced a series of heartwarming Christmas paintings over the years, including the image of an angelic Santa Claus reading his mail in 1935.

Explore the Art of Norman Rockwell

Norman Rockwell Museum ★ *See Norman Rockwell's studio and a museum of his life's work in small-town Stockbridge, Massachusetts.*

The Battle of the Bulge/World War II

The Battle of the Bulge was one of the most significant and costly battles of World War II. It began in December of 1944, when the German Army attacked Allied forces in the Ardennes Forest near the borders of Belgium, Luxembourg, France, and Germany. As the fighting continued on Christmas Day, a small group of American soldiers, lost in the thick forest and one of them wounded, approached a cabin in the woods and knocked at the door. A woman answered and invited the soldiers inside for shelter and a meal with her and her son. According to the son's account, the Americans' rest was soon disturbed by another knock on the door. This time, it was a group of German troops—an extremely dangerous situation for the lost Americans. But the woman came to the Americans' defense. She told the German soldiers they were welcome in her home, but that she would have no violence on Christmas, and insisted they leave their weapons outside. The German soldiers obliged, and joined the woman, her son, and the Americans for a tense but peaceful Christmas dinner before all retired to a night's sleep in the warmth of the cabin. The story was confirmed when the son was reunited with one of the American soldiers decades after the war.

Explore the Battle of the Bulge

Battle of the Bulge Memorial ★ *Visit the memorial at Arlington National Cemetery honoring the nearly twenty thousand Americans killed and fifty thousand wounded in the Battle of the Bulge.*

Ardennes American Cemetery ★ *See the American military cemetery at Liege, Belgium—the final resting place for thousands of American soldiers who died in the Ardennes offensive.*

Christmas in Space on Apollo 8

Less than a month after NASA launched the first American into space in May 1961, President John F. Kennedy set a goal for the U.S. to land men on the moon by the end of the decade. Thousands of small steps toward that goal followed over the next eight years, and one of the most important achievements was Apollo 8, the first manned mission to orbit the moon. Astronauts Frank Borman, Jim Lovell, and Bill Anders entered lunar orbit on December 24, 1968, and became the first people ever to see the moon's surface up close. From orbit, the crew transmitted a Christmas Eve television broadcast, with each astronaut taking turns reading from the Book of Genesis, the biblical story of creation. At the end, Borman signed off, "From the crew of Apollo 8, we close with good night, good luck, a Merry Christmas, and God bless all of you—all of you on the good Earth."

Explore the Apollo Program

National Air and Space Museum ★ *Visit this remarkable museum on the National Mall in Washington, D.C. (and its extraordinary second facility in Chantilly, Virginia), showcasing America's achievements in air and space.*

Johnson Space Center ★ *Tour NASA's Johnson Space Center in Houston, Texas, and see the control room for the Apollo missions.*

America at Christmas is a wonderful place,
full of comfort and joy and the gift of God's grace.
It's a time for remembering what matters the most,
like kindness and faith, and those we keep close.

To my parents, Bernita and Alphonse Bisek,
who taught me the true meaning of Christmas.

★ ★ ★ ★ ★